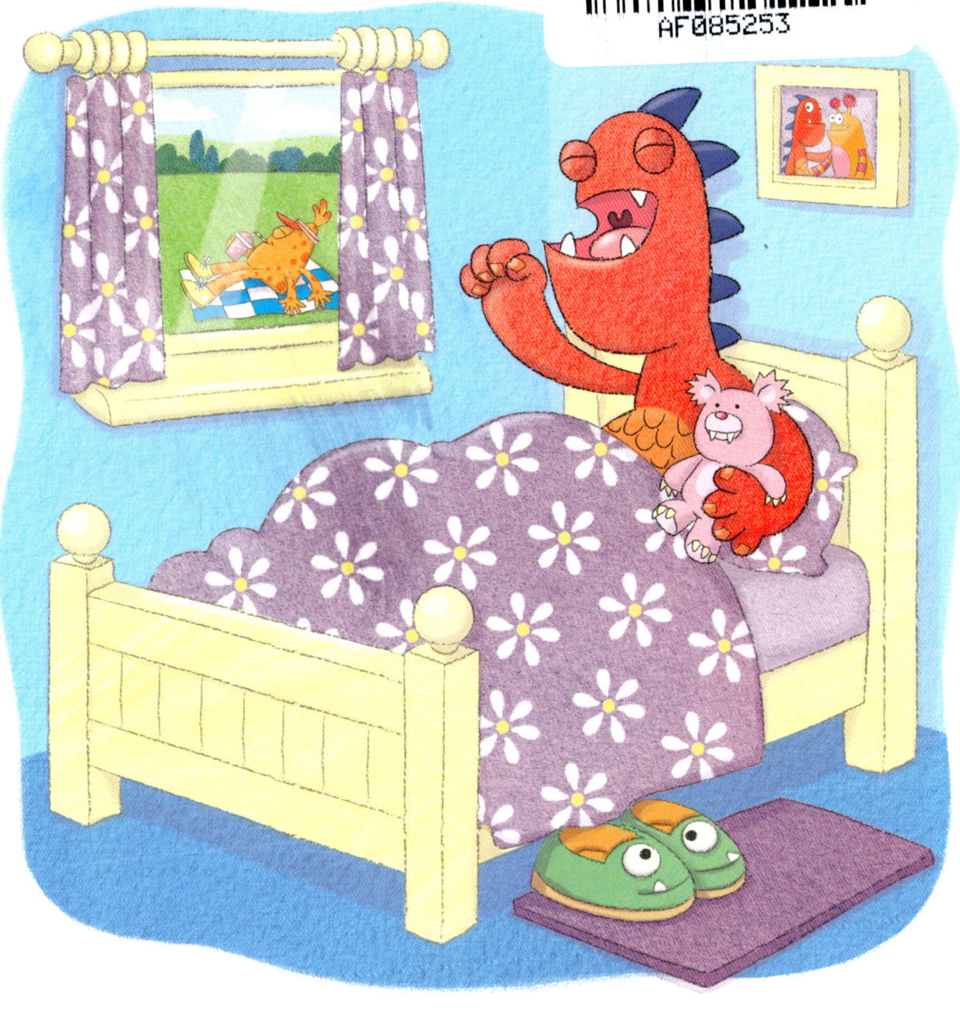

Zed in a bed,

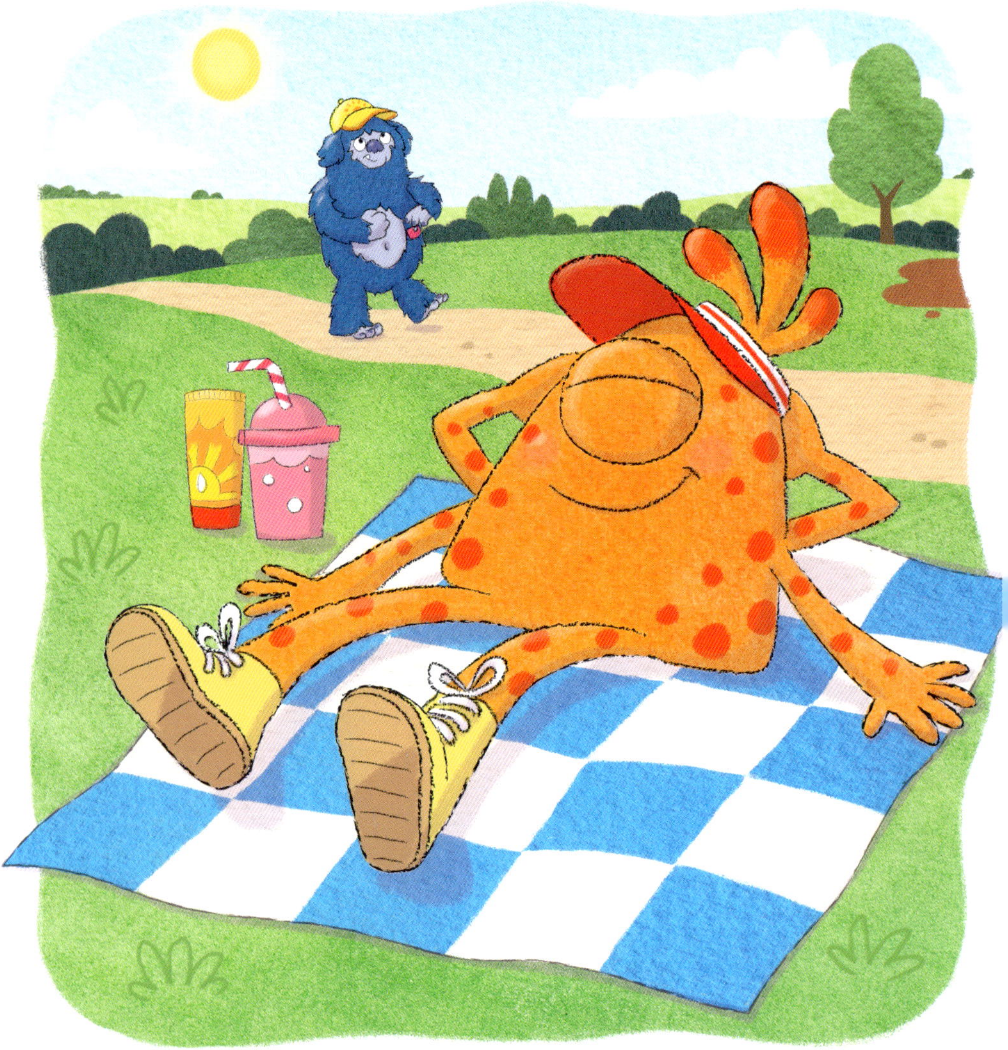

Vun in the sun,

Hap in a cap,

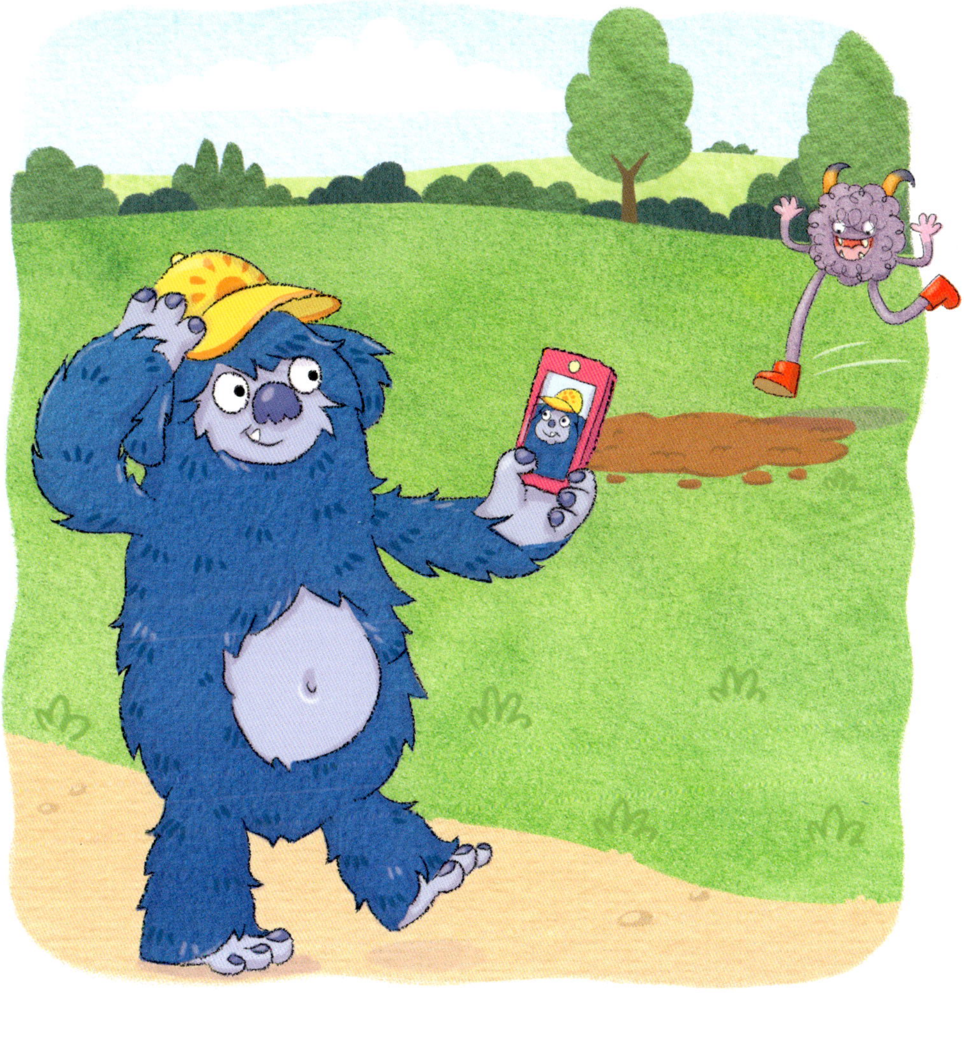

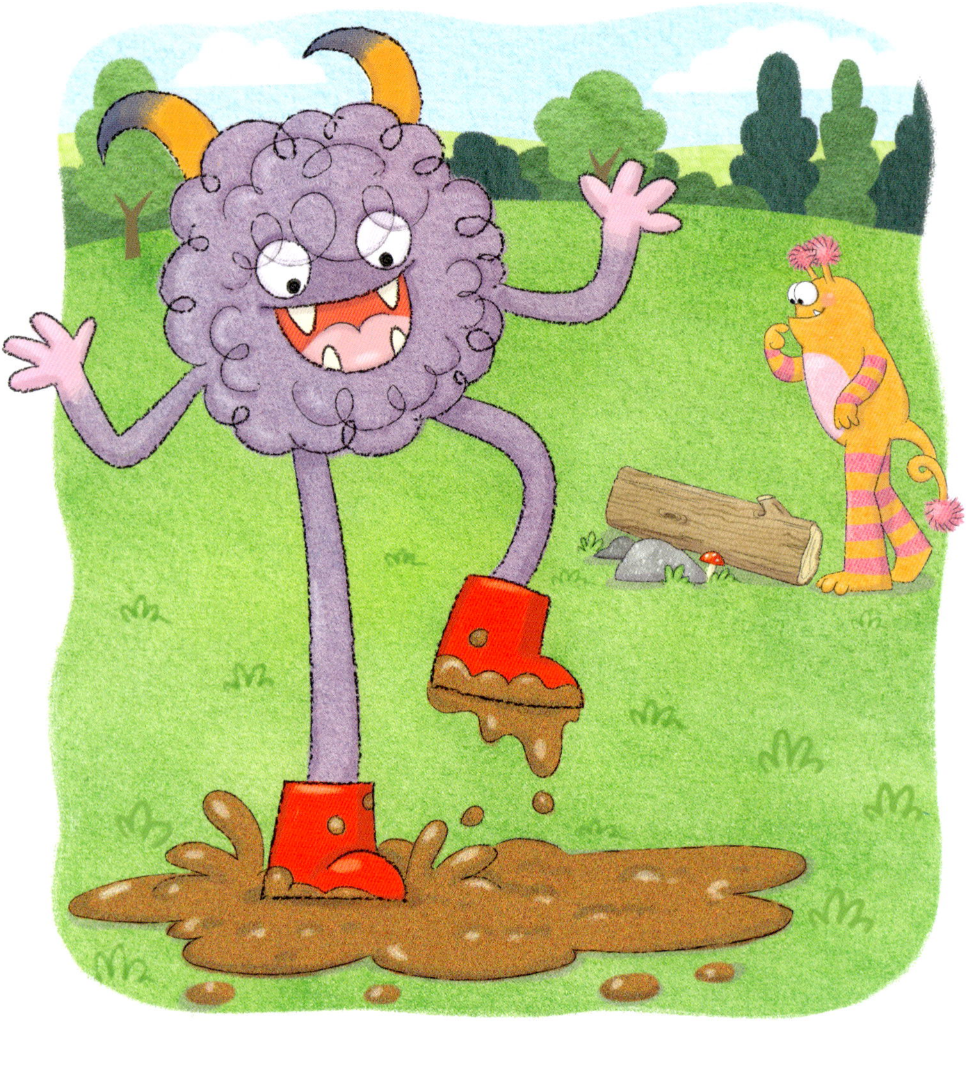

Fud in the mud!

Yog on a log,

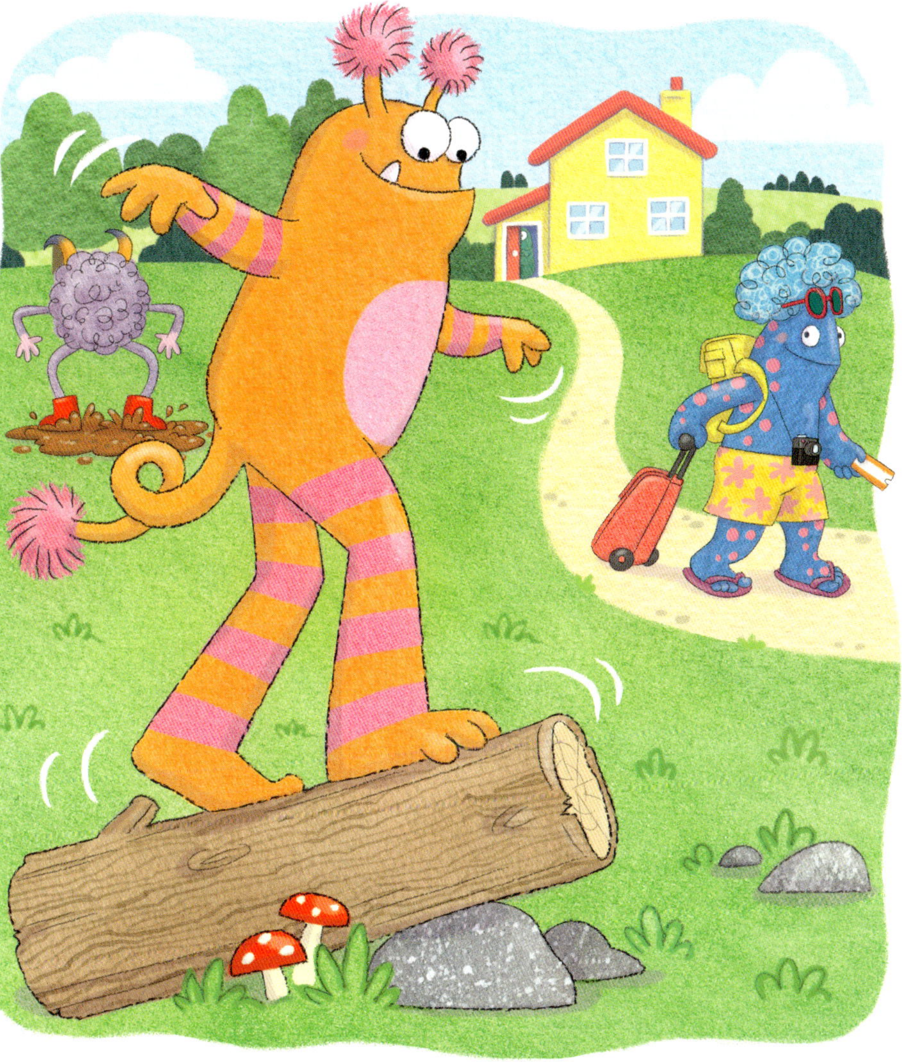

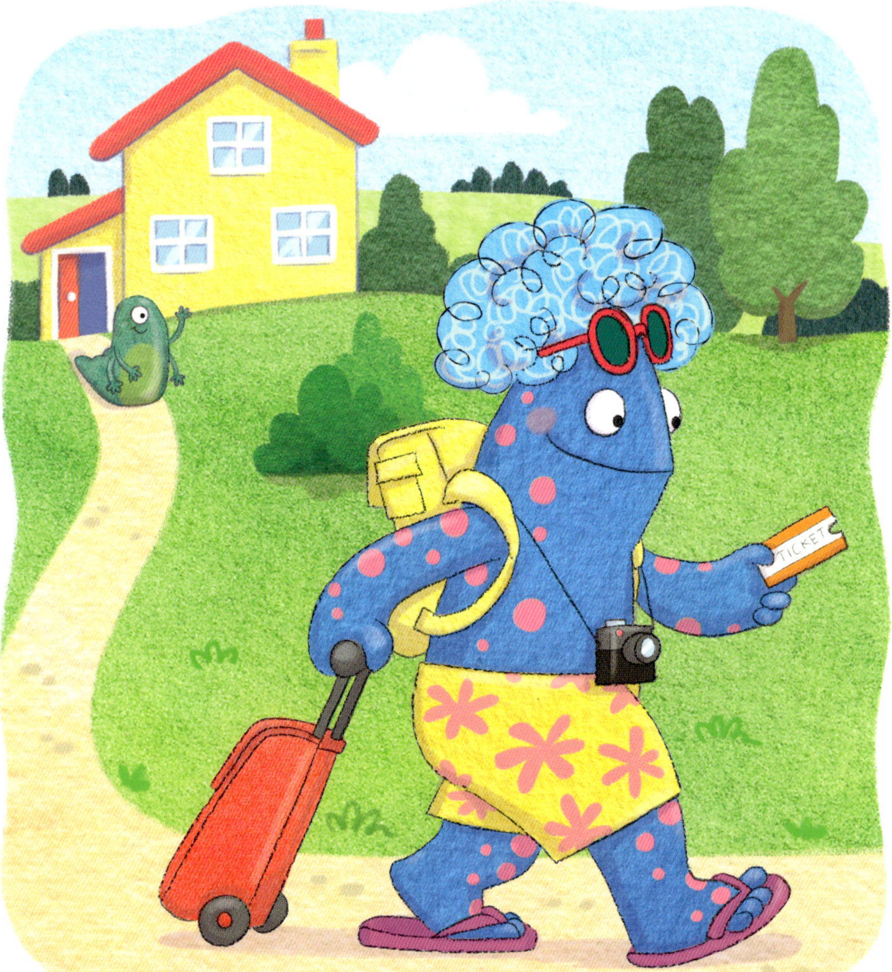

Glip on a trip,

Ren shouts out,
"Ten!"

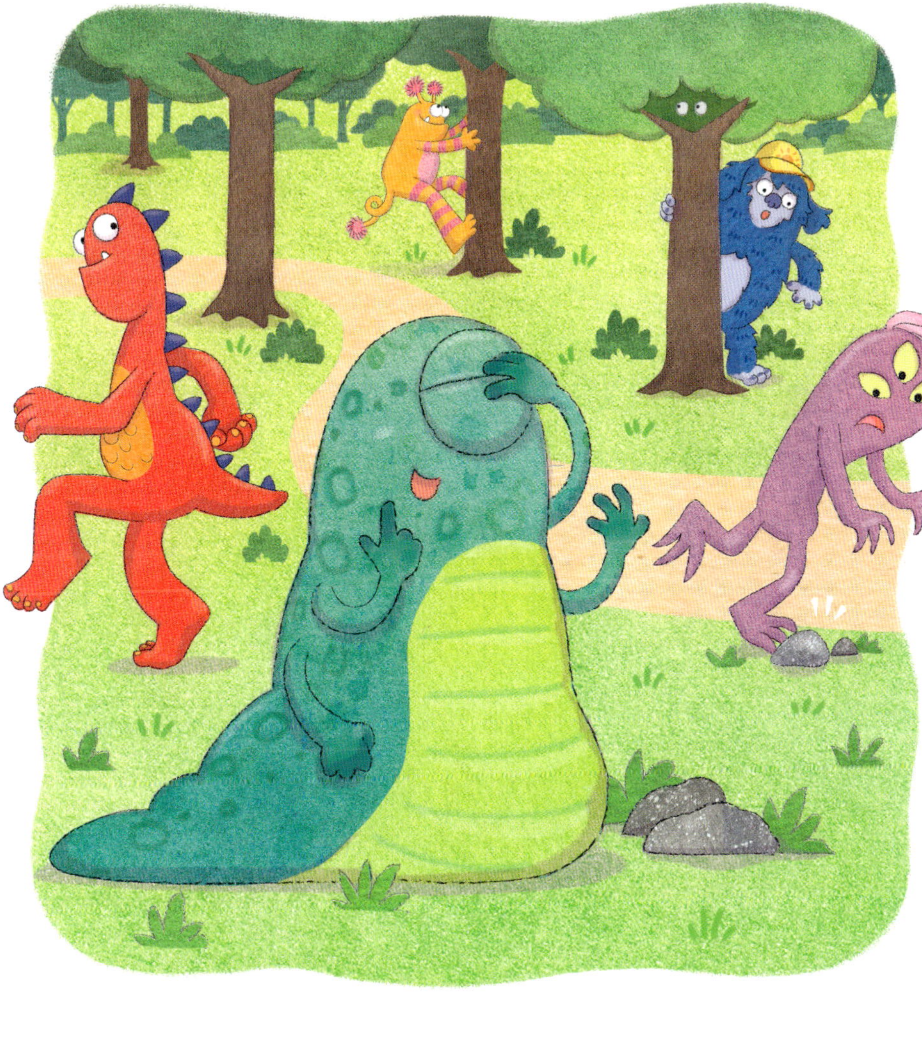

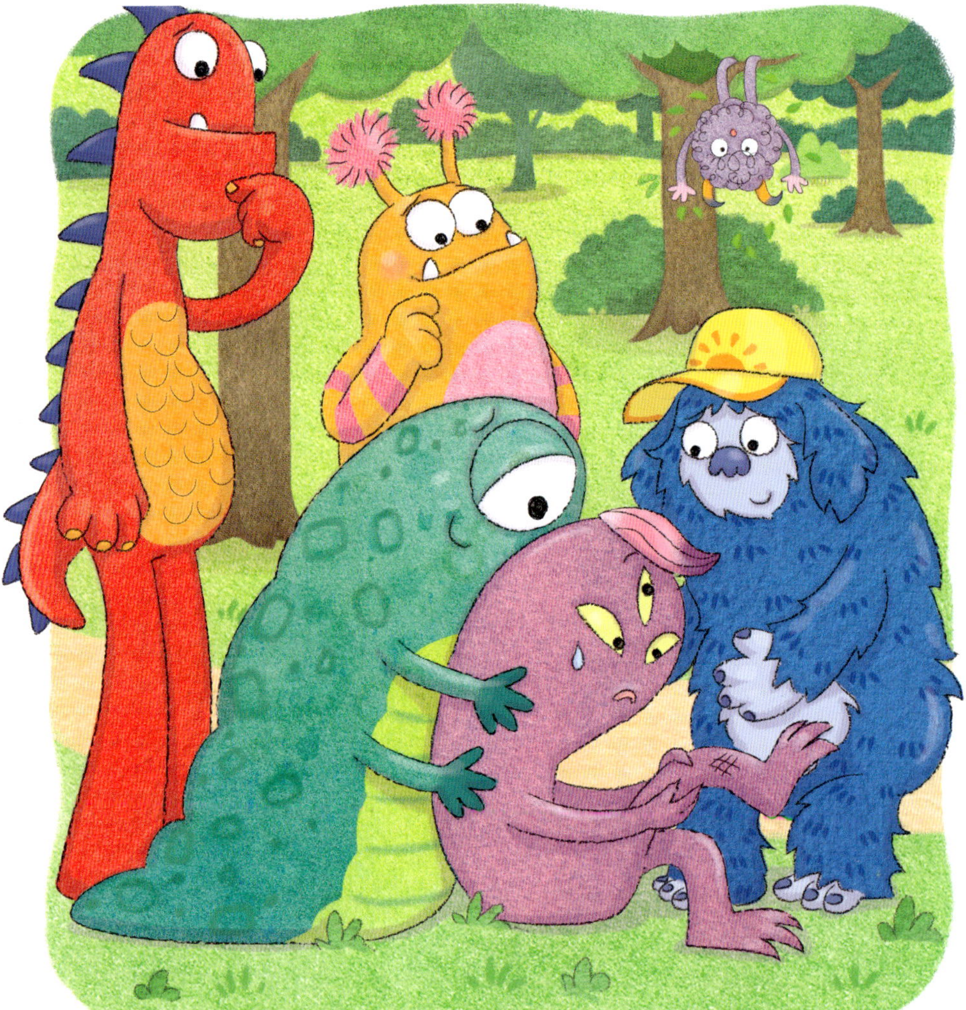

Zug needs a hug!